Defeating the Stigma

Simple Ways to Live a Happy Life

Deepak Singh

ISBN 978-93-5667-705-0
© Deepak Singh 2023

Published in India 2023 by Pencil

A brand of
One Point Six Technologies Pvt. Ltd.
Unit no. 26, Ground Floor, Building A1,
Wadala Truck Terminal Road,
Near Post Office, Antop Hill, Mumbai - 400037
E connect@thepencilapp.com
W www.thepencilapp.com

Author biography

Hello! Happy to meet you, I'm Deepak Singh. I work as a research analyst and am passionate in writing books and doing research on the planet Earth, space, and the art of living. I most likely have high analytical and critical thinking abilities that enable me to assess data, spot trends, and reach conclusions in my capacity as a research analyst. As part of my job, I might perform primary and secondary research, analyse available data, and provide findings to guide individual, corporate, or organisational decision-making. I adore writing and researching about as interests in space and Earth in my free time. You can tell that I have an open mind and am interested in learning about the world around you.

CONTENTS

Chapter 1 Understanding Stigma and Its Consequences.... 7

Chapter 2 Using Awareness and Education to Combat Stigma 16

Chapter 3 Managing Self-Stigma 25

Chapter 4 Increasing Resistance to Stigma 34

Chapter 5 Overcoming Stigma at Work 42

Chapter 6 Getting Around Stigma in Healthcare 50

Chapter 7 Stigma and Personal Relationships 58

Chapter 8 Promoting Good Mental Health 67

Chapter 9 Creating Community Support 77

Chapter 10 Change Advocating 86

Conclusion 94

Introduction

Mental health is an important aspect of our total well-being, although it is sometimes disregarded or stigmatised. The stigma associated with mental health can make it difficult for people to seek help, which can have serious consequences in their life. It is, nevertheless, feasible to overcome the stigma and live a happy life with the correct tools and tactics.

This book is a guidebook that attempts to offer persons dealing with mental health concerns with practical guidance and methods. This book was written by mental health experts with vast expertise dealing with a variety of mental health issues. The writers recognise that mental health is a complex and difficult topic, and they have presented simple yet effective solutions that anyone may use in their daily life.

This book emphasises the need of individual effort, social support, and structural change in combating mental health stigma. It gives individuals practical advice on how to prioritise their mental health, get help when needed, and develop good coping techniques. In addition, the book emphasises the importance of social support from family, friends, and mental health experts in overcoming stigma and living a full life.

Furthermore, structural change is required to eliminate the stigma associated with mental health. As a result, the book provides guidance on how companies, schools, and healthcare providers may foster safe and inclusive settings that prioritise mental health.

Overall, this book is a thorough manual that takes a complete approach to mental health. It is an excellent resource for anyone seeking to overcome stigma and live a full life free of mental health stigma.

Chapter 1 Understanding Stigma and Its Consequences

What exactly is stigma?

- Stigma is a complex social construct that refers to people's unfavorable attitudes and beliefs about specific groups or individuals. It is a process of labeling, categorizing, and discriminating against people based on qualities including race, gender, sexual orientation, health status, mental health, and many more.

- Stigma is not a new phenomenon; it has existed for ages in communities. However, the consequences for individuals who are affected by it can be disastrous. Stigma can result in social marginalization, discrimination, and, in extreme cases, violence. It can also make it difficult for people to access resources and services including healthcare, education, and work, as well as limit their prospects for personal and social development.

- The causes of stigma are varied and vary depending on the situation. Some stigmas, for example, are based on cultural and religious beliefs, whereas others are impacted by political, economic, and historical circumstances. Furthermore, individuals, groups, and institutions, such as the media, healthcare systems, and government laws, can propagate stigma.

- Mental health stigma is one of the most widespread types of stigma. People with mental illnesses are frequently portrayed as violent, unstable, and weak. These preconceptions can cause social isolation and prejudice, as well as discourage people from getting help. The stigma associated with mental health can be especially detrimental, as it can intensify symptoms and delay or prevent rehabilitation.

- Stigma can also be linked to physical health issues. People living with HIV/AIDS, for example, may face stigma and prejudice as a result of misconceptions about the disease. Similarly, people with disabilities may endure stigma as a result of their physical or mental limitations, limiting their access to education, work, and other opportunities.

- Stigma can be especially devastating when it is internalized by those who encounter it. When people begin to believe negative preconceptions and attitudes about themselves, they develop internalized stigma, which can lead to low self-esteem, shame, and other bad results. Internalized stigma can be a substantial impediment to recovery, preventing people from seeking help.

- Stigma reduction is a difficult and continuing process that necessitates education, awareness, and social change. It entails confronting negative preconceptions and attitudes, encouraging empathy and understanding, and advocating for policies and practices that promote inclusion and diversity. Furthermore, eradicating stigma necessitates the participation of everyone, including individuals, communities, and institutions.

To summarise, stigma is a pervasive and detrimental social construct that has a wide-ranging impact on people's lives. It can be linked to a variety of factors, including ethnicity, gender, sexual orientation, health status, and mental health. Stigma can result in social isolation, discrimination, and violence, as well as a lack of access to resources and opportunities. Stigma reduction necessitates a holistic approach that includes education, awareness, and societal change.

Different types of stigma

Stigma is a social phenomenon that can have far-reaching consequences for individuals and society. It refers to people's negative attitudes and opinions about a specific group or individual. Stigma can take many forms and affect many diverse categories of individuals, including those with mental illnesses, disabilities, and marginalized identities. In this article, we will look at the many types of stigma and their impacts.

- **Public stigma:**The most frequent sort of stigma is public stigma, which is defined by negative attitudes and beliefs held by the broader public against a specific group or individual. Discrimination, social marginalization, and unequal treatment can all result from public stigma. Individuals with mental health disorders, for example, may be stigmatized by society, resulting in fewer career possibilities, social isolation, and limited access to healthcare.

- **Self-stigma:**The unfavorable attitudes and ideas that people with stigmatized identities have about themselves are referred to as self-stigma. Low self-esteem, social seclusion, and a lower quality of life can all result from self-stigma. For example, a person suffering from a mental illness may believe that they are weak or imperfect, leading to self-doubt and a lack of confidence in their abilities.

- **Institutional stigma:**When stigmatizing ideas and practices are incorporated into the policies and procedures of organizations and institutions, institutional stigma emerges. Institutional stigma can lead to unequal treatment, a lack of resources, and a lack of opportunity. Policies that discriminate against people with disabilities, for example, might create institutional stigma, resulting in hurdles to education, employment, and healthcare.

- **Structural stigma:**The ways in which societal structures and institutions promote stigma and discrimination are referred to as structural stigma. Structural stigma can result in a scarcity of resources, a lack of opportunity, and social marginalization. Systemic racism, for example, can result in structural stigma, resulting in unequal access to healthcare, education, and career prospects for marginalized communities.

- **Enacted stigma:**Enacted stigma arises when people face discrimination or prejudice because of their stigmatized identity. Stigmatization can lead to social marginalization, reduced opportunities, and severe health outcomes. For example, a disabled person may have physical impediments to accessing public settings, resulting in feelings of social isolation and limited involvement in society.

To summarise, stigma is a complicated and varied phenomenon that can have serious consequences for individuals and communities. Understanding the many types of stigma can aid in addressing the negative attitudes and beliefs that contribute to stigma and discrimination. We may work towards a more inclusive and fair society by combating stigma and fostering acceptance.

Mental health stigma

Individuals' and society's negative views and ideas about people with mental health disorders are referred to as mental health stigma. It can lead to discrimination, prejudice, and even violence against persons suffering from mental illnesses. Stigma is a substantial barrier to mental health care, preventing many people from obtaining necessary assistance. This topic will look at the influence of stigma on mental health and how to eliminate it.

Stigma is described as a mark of shame or disgrace connected with a specific incident or condition. Stigma in the context of mental health can take numerous forms, including discrimination, prejudice, and social exclusion. People suffering from mental illnesses may be seen as weak, dangerous, or unpredictable, which can result in social isolation and exclusion from employment, education, and social activities.

Stigma has a huge impact on mental health. It may discourage people from getting help when they are in need, resulting in more severe symptoms and a longer recovery time. Stigma can also lead to low self-esteem, feelings of humiliation, and a sense of hopelessness, all of which can exacerbate mental health issues.

Discrimination in the employment, school, and healthcare sectors can also result from stigma. People suffering from mental illnesses may face discrimination when looking for work or receiving healthcare, which can lead to financial hardships and social isolation.

Understanding the underlying causes of mental illness is critical for reducing stigma. A lack of awareness and understanding of mental health disorders is one of the primary causes of stigma. People may have unfavorable ideas about mental health because they do not understand the nature of the disorder, its causes, or the treatments available. As a result, education and awareness-raising activities are critical in decreasing the stigma associated with mental health.

Another strategy to lessen the stigma associated with mental health is to promote positive depictions of mental health disorders in the media. People's attitudes and opinions are heavily influenced by the media, and depicting mental health issues in a good light can help eliminate the negative preconceptions associated with them.

Mental health practitioners can also help to reduce the stigma associated with mental illness. Mental health practitioners can assist lessen emotions of guilt and hopelessness, which can exacerbate mental health problems, by fostering a secure and supportive atmosphere for people with mental health conditions.

To summarise, mental health stigma is a substantial barrier to mental health care, preventing many people from obtaining the assistance they require. Stigma can lead to discrimination, prejudice, and social isolation, as well as exacerbate mental health issues. To minimize the stigma associated with mental health, it is critical to promote education, awareness-raising efforts, and good media portrayals of mental health issues. Mental health practitioners can also help to reduce stigma by fostering a friendly environment for those with mental illnesses. We can lessen the stigma associated with mental health by working together to ensure that everyone has access to the care they require.

Individual and societal effects of stigma

Individuals who are stigmatized may have a variety of negative effects, such as sadness, anxiety, social isolation, and low self-esteem. Stigma can cause feelings of shame and worthlessness, making people less inclined to seek help when they are in need. This can aggravate mental health concerns and lead to more serious health issues in the future. Stigma can also cause barriers to work, education, and healthcare, restricting people's options and preventing them from reaching their full potential.

Furthermore, the influence of stigma can be felt across society. Stigmatization of specific groups can lead to increased discrimination, prejudice, social exclusion, and inequality. Stigmatized communities may suffer structural impediments to obtaining school, work, and healthcare, resulting in generational inequity. Stigma can also cause social tensions by pitting groups against each other in a quest for resources and social prestige.

Mental health is one area where stigma has a particularly large influence. Despite growing public awareness of the mental illness, stigma continues to be a substantial impediment to seeking help and receiving effective treatment. Stigma can make it difficult for people to share their mental health difficulties with others, leading to feelings of isolation and shame. This, in turn, can exacerbate mental health concerns and make it more difficult to successfully treat symptoms. Stigma can also lead to a shortage of resources for mental health care, such as financing for research and healthcare professional training.

Stigma's impact on society is not confined to mental health. Stigma can also harm marginalized groups, such as the poor and those with impairments. These people may confront a lack of access to education, healthcare, and work prospects, making it difficult for them to break free from the cycle of poverty. Long-term social and economic inequities might result, in sustaining a cycle of deprivation that affects generations.

To summarise, stigma is a widespread problem with far-reaching consequences for both individuals and society. It can result in poor mental health, social marginalization, and economic deprivation. To address stigma, all levels of society, including individuals, community organizations, and policymakers, must work together. We can create a more inclusive and equitable society for all by working together to fight negative attitudes and ideas.

Chapter 2 Using Awareness and Education to Combat Stigma

The significance of education and awareness:

- Awareness and education are two of the most effective strategies to eliminate stigma. We can minimize the prevalence and impact of stigma by raising people's understanding of its sources and effects.

- To begin, education can assist in dispelling beliefs and prejudices that lead to stigma. Because of a lack of awareness or exposure, many people have unfavorable beliefs about groups they consider to be different. For example, mental health stigma is frequently founded on the incorrect idea that people suffering from mental illnesses are dangerous or unpredictable. We can fight these beliefs and create more positive attitudes towards persons with mental health disorders by sharing factual information about mental health and mental illness.

- Second, raising awareness can aid in breaking down the secrecy and shame that frequently surround stigmatized conditions or identities.

Many people who are stigmatized may feel alienated and unsupported, which can have a severe influence on their mental health and well-being. We can eliminate shame and promote a more inclusive and tolerant society by bringing these concerns into the light and creating safe spaces for discussion and support.

- Finally, education and awareness can help to improve access to resources and support for persons who are stigmatized. Many persons who are stigmatized may suffer challenges to healthcare, work, or social support as a result of discrimination or social exclusion. We may strive towards a more just and inclusive society by raising awareness of these concerns and lobbying for more equal policies and services.

Finally, stigma awareness and education are critical for developing a more equal and inclusive society. We can lessen the negative impact of stigma on individuals and communities by questioning misconceptions and stereotypes, creating safe spaces for conversation and support, and lobbying for more fair policies and services. Let us all endeavor to be more aware, empathetic, and tolerant of those who are different from us, and work towards a society in which stigma has no power over people's lives.

What you can do to educate yourself and others

To foster a more inclusive and equitable society, we must educate ourselves and others about stigma.

Here are some ideas for educating yourself and others about stigma:

- **Grasp the causes and repercussions of stigma:**In order to effectively teach others about stigma, you must first grasp what it is and the numerous variables that contribute to it. Stigma can be based on a variety of variables, such as ethnicity, gender, sexual orientation, mental health, or physical disability. It can take numerous forms, including bullying, discrimination, and social isolation. It is critical to comprehend the various types of stigma and how they affect individuals and society.

- **Teach oneself about the experiences of stigmatized groups:**In order to effectively teach others about stigma, you must first comprehend the experiences of stigmatized groups. This can include reading books and articles, viewing documentaries and movies, and interacting with members of marginalized groups. Learning about other people's experiences can help you develop empathy and understanding, which can help you become a stronger advocate for those who face stigma.

- **Examine your own prejudices and assumptions:**When it comes to stigma, it is critical to examine your own biases and assumptions. We all have biases about certain categories of individuals, and it is critical to recognize these biases and fight to eradicate them.

One method is to engage in self-reflection and question why you hold certain views or assumptions.

- **Engage in an open and honest dialogue:**Speaking openly and honestly about stigma can be an effective method to educate people. By honestly discussing your own experiences and points of view, you can encourage others to do the same. It is critical to creating a comfortable and non-judgmental environment for these discussions to take place. You can also utilize these interactions to dispel myths and preconceptions.

- **Use inclusive and courteous language:**Language can play an important role in the perpetuation of stigma. When discussing stigmatized communities, it is critical to utilize inclusive and courteous language. This includes avoiding pejorative terminology and employing person-first language, which emphasizes the individual rather than their condition or identity. Instead of "a schizophrenic person," you may say "a person with schizophrenia."

- **Encourage positive representations:**Promoting positive images of stigmatized communities is another technique to educate others about stigma. This can include telling the tales of people who have overcome stigma or emphasizing the accomplishments of stigmatized communities. You may counter negative preconceptions and promote a more positive perspective of these communities by displaying positive portrayals.

To summarise, stigma is a widespread social problem that can have a catastrophic influence on the lives of individuals who experience it. It is critical to educate yourself and others about stigma in order to promote a more inclusive and equal society. Understanding the causes and effects of stigma, confronting your own biases, engaging in open and honest dialogues, adopting the inclusive language, and supporting positive portrayals may all contribute to a more supportive and accepting society for all.

Examples of effective anti-stigma initiatives

Stigma is a significant impediment to advancement, causing people to suffer in secret, delay seeking aid, or even give up on life. To counteract the detrimental consequences of stigma, several anti-stigma efforts have been established over the years. Here are some examples of successful anti-stigma efforts that have benefited society.

- **It's Time to Change:**Time to Change is a 2007 anti-stigma campaign headquartered in the United Kingdom. It is a collaboration between Mind and Rethinks Mental Illness, two renowned mental health organizations. The campaign aims to influence people's attitudes and behaviors toward mental health by confronting negative perceptions and attitudes. Time to Change employs a number of strategies, including advertising, social media, events, and collaborations with corporations and schools. The program has touched millions of individuals and has been helpful in decreasing the stigma surrounding mental health.

- **Let's Talk, Bell:**Bell Let's Talk is a Canadian mental health campaign that began in 2010. It is an annual campaign that encourages people to discuss mental health openly and raises awareness of mental health issues. The campaign has a strong social media presence and encourages individuals to share their stories and experiences using the hashtag #BellLetsTalk. Bell Let's Talk has been successful in reducing mental health stigma and has raised more than $100 million for mental health projects.

- **Beyond the Blue:**Beyond Blue is a non-profit organization based in Australia that was founded in 2000. Its mission is to improve the lives of people who suffer from anxiety, despair, and suicidal ideation. Beyond Blue has created a number of effective anti-stigma programs, including the "Stop. Think. Respect." campaign, which attempts to minimize discrimination against persons suffering from mental illnesses. The campaign challenges negative preconceptions and encourages people to think differently about mental health through television, radio, print, and online advertising.

- **It Will Get Better Project:**The It Gets Better Project is a non-profit organization based in the United States that was founded in 2010. Its mission is to prevent suicide among LGBTQ+ kids by offering support and encouragement. The campaign includes videos of celebrities, politicians, and everyday people sharing their stories and offering words of encouragement to LGBTQ+ youngsters. The It Gets Better Project has been successful in decreasing stigma and giving LGBTQ+ youth a sense of community and support.

- **The Special Olympics Games:**The Special Olympics is an international sports training and competition organization for people with intellectual disabilities. The Special Olympics has sponsored various anti-stigma projects, including the "Spread the Word to End the Word" campaign, which attempts to eliminate the usage of the slur "retard" as a derogatory term. The campaign raises awareness of the damaging impacts of the phrase and promotes respect and inclusion for persons with intellectual impairments through social media, events, and collaborations with schools and companies.

Finally, these are only a few examples of successful anti-stigma initiatives that have had a good social influence. These efforts have worked to reduce prejudice, increase inclusion, and enhance the lives of people impacted by stigma by confronting negative attitudes and preconceptions. To develop a more welcoming and caring society, it is critical to continue to support and promote anti-stigma efforts.

The function of the media in combating stigma

Stigma can be exceedingly damaging, causing discrimination, prejudice, and marginalization. Those who encounter it may also endure feelings of humiliation, self-doubt, and low self-esteem.

The media, in all of its forms, shapes people's perceptions and attitudes toward a variety of topics, including stigma. The media has the ability to combat stigma, dispel misconceptions, and foster understanding and acceptance of marginalized communities.

One of the most important methods for the media to counter stigma is to provide truthful information about the problem at hand. When it comes to mental health stigma, for example, the media may play an important role in educating people about the reality of mental health issues, their causes, and the treatments that are available. The media can help to eliminate myths and preconceptions by giving factual and accessible information, which can lead to more understanding and less stigma.

The media can also help to combat stigma by presenting positive portrayals of marginalized communities. In recent years, for example, we have witnessed more representation of marginalized communities in popular cultures, such as people of color, LGBTQ+ people, and persons with disabilities. This portrayal can aid in the dismantling of preconceptions and the promotion of understanding and acceptance of these groups. Witnessing good images of marginalized communities in the media can enable them to overcome negative perceptions and stigma.

Another option for the media to combat stigma is to expose the lives and experiences of those who have faced stigma and discrimination. Sharing experiences of those who have overcome stigma and discrimination, as well as those who are still battling, can be part of this. By exposing these experiences, the media can assist to humanise the issue and demonstrate that it is more than simply an abstract concept affecting actual people.

Finally, the media may challenge stigma by facilitating discourse and discussion about the topic. Media outlets, for example, can arrange panel discussions, debates, and town hall meetings on stigma concerns. These gatherings can provide a forum for people to express their experiences and viewpoints, as well as for the general public to learn about and participate in the subject.

To summarize, the media can play a significant role in combating stigma. The media may help to break down preconceptions, improve understanding, and eventually minimize the destructive impact of stigma on marginalized communities by giving factual information, supporting positive representation, spotlighting human stories, and generating chances for debate. Media outlets must recognize their power and duty and use their platforms to combat stigma in all of its manifestations.

Chapter 3 Managing Self-Stigma

What exactly is self-stigma?

When a person has been stigmatized by society, healthcare providers, or even family members, they begin to believe the bad labels that have been placed on them. Negative self-talk can result in low self-esteem, despair, anxiety, and hopelessness.

A person suffering from a mental health problem, for example, may feel humiliated and guilty about their disease, which they regard as a weakness or character flaw. They may even believe they are unworthy of love, respect, or achievement. This self-stigma might make it difficult for people to seek therapy, socialize, or pursue their goals and objectives.

Self-stigma can also contribute to poor self-care, such as ignoring physical health, avoiding exercise or a good diet, or failing to take prescribed medication as instructed. This can exacerbate their physical and mental health problems, creating a vicious cycle of self-stigma, bad health, and low self-esteem.

Education and awareness are two of the most effective strategies to prevent self-stigma. Individuals suffering from self-stigma must understand that their diseases are not their fault and that there is no shame in seeking therapy or help. It's also crucial to recognize that many successful and talented people have struggled with mental health issues and that mental health issues are common and curable medical conditions.

Self-stigma can also be addressed through support groups, counseling, and therapy. Individuals can use these tools to talk about their experiences, acquire coping methods, and build resilience. Peer support groups can also be beneficial because they allow people to connect with others who have had similar struggles and create a sense of community and belonging.

To summarise, self-stigma is a damaging internalization of society's negative views and attitudes towards a specific group of individuals. Low self-esteem, despair, anxiety, and a lack of self-care might result. Individuals can battle self-stigma via education, awareness, and seeking support, allowing them to live a full life despite any obstacles they may experience.

The impact of self-stigma on mental health

Self-stigma is a phenomenon that arises when an individual internalizes and embraces society's negative stereotypes and prejudices against a specific group. Individuals who encounter mental health disorders frequently internalize the stigma associated with these conditions, leading to self-stigma. As it can have a negative influence on mental health, self-stigma is a significant barrier to seeking help and receiving proper treatment.

Self-stigma has a variety of effects on mental health. For starters, it can result in lower self-esteem and self-worth. Individuals who internalize the stigma associated with mental health disorders may come to believe that they are less important or deserving of respect and assistance. This can lead to feelings of shame and inadequacy, which can aggravate mental health issues including melancholy and anxiety.

Second, social isolation and loneliness can result from self-stigma. Individuals who internalize stigma may avoid social situations or interactions with others because they are ashamed or embarrassed about their condition. This might lead to a loss of social support, which is necessary for optimal mental health.

Third, self-stigma might make it difficult to seek aid and treatment. Individuals who internalize unfavorable preconceptions about mental health disorders may assume that seeking treatment is a sign of weakness or failure. Delays in obtaining therapy can aggravate mental health disorders and make them more difficult to address.

Finally, self-stigma can contribute to feelings of hopelessness and despair. Individuals who internalize the stigma associated with mental health disorders may assume that their disease is permanent and that they will never fully recover. This might lead to a lack of drive to engage in activities or seek therapy, exacerbating mental health issues.

It is critical to recognize that self-stigma is a substantial obstacle to receiving effective care for mental health disorders. To overcome self-stigma, a mix of self-reflection, education, and support is required. Individuals can confront their negative attitudes and thoughts regarding mental health issues by gathering factual information, engaging in self-care activities, and seeking assistance from mental health experts or support groups.

To summarise, self-stigma is a widespread problem that has a variety of consequences for mental health. Overcoming self-stigma is critical for individuals to receive the necessary therapy and support to preserve their mental health. Individuals can overcome self-stigma and obtain improved mental health outcomes by questioning negative attitudes and seeking support.

Methods for Overcoming Self-Stigma

Self-stigma refers to the unfavorable attitudes and ideas that people have about themselves as a result of being stigmatized for personal qualities such as their mental health, race, gender, sexual orientation, or physical ability. Self-stigma can cause emotions of shame, guilt, and inferiority, all of which can have a negative impact on an individual's mental and emotional well-being. Fortunately, there are strategies available to assist individuals in overcoming self-stigma and regaining self-esteem and self-worth.

Here are some successful methods for overcoming self-stigma:

- **Education and Public Awareness:**Education and awareness are two of the most effective strategies to combat self-stigma. This entails learning more about the personal characteristics for which you have been stigmatized, as well as comprehending the fundamental causes and effects of stigma on mental and emotional well-being. You can gain a better awareness of yourself and the world around you by being more informed, which can assist to lessen negative self-judgment and improve self-acceptance.

- **CBT stands for Cognitive Behavioural Therapy:**CBT is a method of psychotherapy that aims to alter harmful thought patterns and beliefs. It can assist people in overcoming self-stigma by identifying and confronting negative self-talk and beliefs. Individuals can build more positive and realistic self-perceptions by reframing negative thoughts and beliefs, which can improve their overall mental and emotional well-being.

- **Mindfulness:**Mindfulness is a strategy that involves paying attention to the current moment without judgment. It can help people overcome self-stigma by enhancing self-awareness and decreasing negative self-talk. Individuals can learn to examine their thoughts and feelings without judgment by practicing mindfulness, which can help to minimize feelings of shame and guilt.

- **Social Support:**Social support is critical in overcoming self-stigma. It entails searching out helpful persons who can offer both emotional and practical assistance. Family members, friends, and mental health experts can all be included. Social support can help to alleviate feelings of loneliness while also increasing sentiments of acceptance and belonging.

- **Self-Care:**Self-care is a critical strategy for combating self-stigma. It entails doing things that enhance physical, mental, and emotional well-being. This can include physical activity, a good diet, relaxation techniques, and hobbies. Individuals can improve their general well-being and self-worth by prioritizing self-care.

To summarise, eradicating self-stigma takes patience, persistence, and self-compassion. Individuals can learn to overcome negative self-judgment and reclaim their self-esteem and self-worth by utilizing approaches such as education and awareness, cognitive behavioral therapy, mindfulness, social support, and self-care. Remember, it is appropriate to ask for help and support during this process, and it is possible to overcome self-stigma and live a full life with time and effort.

Self-affirmation and positive self-talk

Positive self-talk and affirmations are effective methods for cultivating a positive mentality and improving general well-being. The way we speak to ourselves has a big influence on our ideas, feelings, and behaviors. We can adjust our perspective and build a more optimistic outlook on life by using positive words and affirmations.

What exactly is positive self-talk?

The practice of utilizing encouraging and uplifting words to connect with oneself is known as positive self-talk. It entails intentionally choosing positive ideas and affirmations over negative or critical self-talk. Motivational phrases, encouraging statements, and positive self-affirmations are all examples of positive self-talk.

Why is it important to have positive self-talk?

Our emotions and behavior can be greatly influenced by our thoughts and beliefs. We reinforce limiting ideas and negative thought patterns when we engage in negative self-talk, which can lead to emotions of worry, self-doubt, and sadness. Positive self-talk, on the other hand, can assist us in developing a more resilient and optimistic mindset, which can improve our general mental health and well-being.

The Advantages of Positive Self-Talk:

- **Reduces tension and Anxiety:**By providing a more positive and optimistic perspective on difficult events, positive self-talk can help reduce tension and anxiety.

- **Boosts Confidence:**Positive affirmations can help increase self-confidence and self-esteem, leading to a more positive attitude toward life.

- **Improves Mood:**Focusing on positive thoughts and affirmations can enhance mood and alleviate depressive symptoms.

- **Enhances Resilience:**Positive self-talk can assist build resilience by encouraging and motivating you during challenging moments.

- **Promotes Goal Setting:**Positive self-talk can help us set and achieve objectives by instilling confidence in our abilities to succeed.

Positive Self-Talk Techniques:

- **Start with Awareness:**Begin by becoming conscious of your internal conversation and becoming aware of any negative or critical self-talk.

- **Positive Thoughts Should Replace Negative Thoughts:**Replace negative self-talk with positive affirmations or encouraging words when you recognize it.

- **Use the present tense:**When affirming yourself, use present tense words. Say "I am confident and capable" instead of "I will be confident and capable."

- **Repeat Daily:**Make positive affirmations and self-talk a part of your everyday practice. Remind yourself of them on a frequent basis to promote positive attitudes and cognitive patterns.

Positive Affirmations Examples:

- I am capable of reaching my objectives.

- I am deserving of love and respect.

- I am self-assured and confident.

- I have faith in my capacity to make sound

- I am thankful for all of my blessings.

Finally, positive self-talk and affirmations can be an effective strategy for cultivating a positive mindset and improving general well-being. We can adjust our viewpoint and acquire a more optimistic outlook on life by paying attention to our internal dialogue and intentionally choosing to focus on positive thoughts and affirmations. Positive self-talk can become a habit that helps us negotiate life's problems with perseverance, confidence, and grace with practice.

Chapter 4 Increasing Resistance to Stigma

What exactly is resilience?

Resilience is the ability to adapt to and recover from adversity. It is the ability to recover from adversity, overcome obstacles, and retain a good attitude in the face of setbacks. People are not born with resilience; rather, it is a quality that can be learned and developed through experience and practice.

Resilience is critical for our mental and emotional health. Life is unpredictably unpredictable, and we will all face difficulties and disappointments at some point. Those who are resilient, on the other hand, are better suited to deal with these problems and emerge stronger and more confident.

Resilience is about more than just enduring hardship; it is about learning and growing from those experiences as well. Individuals that are resilient are open to new viewpoints and ideas, and they are willing to change their behavior and thinking in order to improve their condition.

Building strong social relationships, practicing mindfulness and self-care, creating reasonable objectives, and maintaining a positive mentality are all ways to promote resilience. Having a support system of family, friends, or colleagues who can provide emotional and practical help through difficult times is one of the most important components of growing resilience.

According to research, resilience is a strong predictor of success in both personal and professional settings. Resilient people are better equipped to negotiate difficult situations, cope with stress, and keep a sense of purpose and meaning in their life.

One of the most important qualities of resilience is the ability to be cheerful and hopeful. Individuals that are resilient think they have control over their lives and are willing to take action to change their condition. They understand that setbacks are only transitory and that they have the strength and resources to overcome them.

Finally, resilience is an important attribute that may be cultivated via experience and practice. It enables us to overcome adversity, grow and learn from adversity, and retain an optimistic attitude in life. Developing resilience takes time and commitment, but it is an investment in our mental and emotional well-being that may pay off handsomely in all aspects of our life.

The Significance of Resilience in the Face of Stigma

Stigma is a mark of shame or disgrace connected with a specific incident, quality, or person. It is frequently founded in cultural attitudes and can lead to stigmatization and marginalization of individuals. Overcoming stigma necessitates resilience, or the ability to adapt and recover from challenging or unpleasant events.

Because stigmatized persons frequently experience challenges and hurdles that might damage their mental and emotional well-being, resilience is critical in overcoming stigma. Individuals with resilience are able to overcome these problems and create a positive attitude in life. It assists individuals in dealing with stress, developing self-esteem and confidence, and gaining control over their lives.

Having a solid support system, practicing self-care, engaging in activities that bring joy and purpose, and establishing a positive mentality are all ways to build resilience. These tactics can assist individuals in overcoming negative feelings and attitudes connected with stigma and in developing resilience to face obstacles.

Cultivating a sense of community and belonging is one of the most effective methods to increase resilience. Connecting with people who have had similar experiences and sharing tales and techniques for overcoming stigma might help. Seeking help from friends, family, or mental health specialists is another option.

Self-care is another crucial part of growing resilience. Meditation, exercise, and self-reflection are examples of such activities. Self-care activities can help people gain control over their lives and create the resilience needed to overcome the harmful impacts of stigma.

Developing a positive mindset is also essential for resilience strengthening. It entails focusing on one's strengths and skills rather than one's flaws and limitations. Positive thinking can help people build a sense of optimism and hope, which can be especially beneficial in overcoming the challenges and obstacles that come with a stigma.

Finally, resilience is an important aspect of overcoming stigma. It assists people to create a positive view of life, cope with stress, and gain control over their lives. Developing resilience can include a variety of tactics such as cultivating a feeling of community, practicing self-care, and maintaining a positive mindset. Stigmatized people can overcome the harmful consequences of stigma and live satisfying and meaningful lives through developing resilience.

Self-care and healthy coping skills help to build resilience

Resilience is an important life trait to have since it allows us to navigate through difficult circumstances and emerge stronger on the other side. Resilience, on the other hand, is a talent that can be developed over time through self-care and appropriate coping practices.

Self-care is the practice of looking after oneself on all levels: physically, psychologically, and emotionally. It entails creating time for activities that allow us to unwind, refuel, and de-stress. Activities for self-care might be as easy as going for a stroll, reading a book, or listening to music. Self-care activities must be prioritized because they are critical for strengthening resilience and preventing burnout.

Here are some suggestions for increasing resilience through self-care and healthy coping mechanisms:

- **Prioritize self-care:**Make time for things that will help you relax, refuel, and minimize stress. This could involve physical activity, time spent in nature, reading a book, or spending time with loved ones. Remember that self-care is not selfish; it is necessary for your health.

- **Practice mindfulness:**The practice of being present at the moment and conscious of your thoughts and sensations is known as mindfulness. It is a helpful technique for stress management and resilience building. Mindfulness can be practiced through meditation, breathing exercises, or simply focusing on your breath for a few minutes.

- **Practice gratitude:**Gratitude is the practice of focusing on and being appreciative of the good things in one's life. It is a powerful tool for increasing resilience and decreasing stress. Gratitude can be practiced by maintaining a gratitude book or simply taking a few minutes each day to focus on what you are grateful for.

- **Build a support network:**Having a support network of family, friends, or coworkers can be a helpful tool in developing resilience. When you need it the most, they can offer emotional support, advice, and a listening ear.

- **Develop healthy coping strategies:**Building resilience requires healthy coping mechanisms. Exercise, meditation, deep breathing, and talking to a therapist are examples of such activities. It is critical to develop healthy coping mechanisms that work for you and incorporate them into your daily routine.

- **Set realistic goals:**Setting realistic goals is a critical component of developing resilience. It is critical to developing goals that are both demanding and attainable. As you strive towards your goals, this might help you create confidence and resilience.

- **Practice self-compassion:**Self-compassion is the practice of being compassionate and understanding to oneself. It entails being gentle with oneself when you make errors and recognizing your own strengths and flaws. Self-compassion can be a powerful strategy for increasing resilience and decreasing stress.

To summarise, developing resilience via self-care and healthy coping methods is a critical component of living a happy, healthy life. You may build the resilience needed to overcome life's obstacles and emerge stronger on the other side by prioritizing self-care, practicing mindfulness and gratitude, creating healthy coping methods, setting realistic objectives, and practicing self-compassion.

Obtaining assistance from friends, family, and professionals

Individuals' mental health, self-esteem, and overall well-being can all suffer as a result of stigma. Seeking help from friends, family, and professionals can be an important step in overcoming stigma.

When dealing with stigma, friends, and family can be a great source of support. They can offer emotional support, a listening ear, and a safe location to vent one's emotions. It is critical to confide in people who are compassionate and nonjudgmental. To begin, identify trusted individuals and convey the scenario to them. Sharing one's experiences and feelings can be cathartic and beneficial to one's sense of community.

Therapists, counselors, and mental health specialists can also be valuable sources of assistance. They have been taught to create a safe and supportive atmosphere for individuals coping with mental health challenges and stigma. They can provide guidance, validation, and assistance in developing coping methods. Therapy can help people explore their feelings and experiences in order to gain a better understanding of themselves.

There are other mental health and stigma support groups and organizations. These groups can foster a sense of community and understanding, as well as connect individuals with others who have had similar experiences. Individuals can share their stories, seek help, and build coping methods in a safe and nonjudgmental environment through support groups.

When seeking help, keep in mind that everyone's experiences are different, and what works for one person may not work for another. It is also critical to seek help from people who are compassionate and nonjudgmental. Stigma may be a challenging issue to overcome, and seeking help is an important step in dealing with its consequences.

Finally, stigma can have a substantial impact on a person's mental health and well-being. Seeking help from friends, family, and professionals can be an important step in overcoming stigma. It is critical to confide in people who are empathetic and nonjudgmental, as well as to seek out support groups and organizations that are concerned with mental health and stigma. Remember that seeking assistance is a sign of strength, not weakness.

Chapter 5 Overcoming Stigma at Work

The Influence of workplace stigma

Unfortunately, stigma extends beyond social interactions and can be present in the workplace. Stigma in the workplace can have a major and far-reaching influence on both individuals and organisations. In this topic, we will look at the influence of stigma in the workplace and how to deal with it.

Stigma in the workplace can take several forms depending on the situation and the individual or group being stigmatised. Individuals may be stigmatised because of their gender, sexual orientation, race, ethnicity, handicap, or mental health condition, for example. When people are stigmatised at work, it can have an impact on their job chances, career advancement, and even their mental health.

One of the most serious consequences of stigma in the workplace is discrimination. Discrimination can manifest itself in a variety of ways, such as harassment, bullying, or exclusion from social events. This can make it difficult for employees to feel included and valued at work, hurting job satisfaction and productivity. Furthermore, prejudice can lead to employees quitting or being fired, thus limiting workplace diversity and potentially harming the organization's bottom line.

Stigma can also have an impact on people's mental health at work. Individuals who suffer stigma are more likely to have anxiety, sadness, and other mental health issues, according to research. Furthermore, when employees do not feel safe or comfortable at work, it can lead to increased stress and burnout, negatively impacting their overall health and well-being.

Stigma in the workplace can also have an impact on organisations. When there is discrimination and exclusion, it can lead to lower production, lower morale, and higher turnover rates. Furthermore, organisations that do not address workplace stigma may be regarded as unwelcoming and less appealing to potential employees, hurting their capacity to attract and retain diverse talent.

Organisations can take many initiatives to address the impact of stigma in the workplace. First, they can foster an inclusive and respectful culture in which all persons are recognised and acknowledged for their distinct traits. This can be accomplished through diversity and inclusion-promoting training programmes, policies, and processes. Organisations can also provide resources and support to employees who are stigmatised, such as mental health services, employee assistance programmes, and support groups.

Additionally, organisations can try to address any structural issues that may contribute to workplace stigma. For example, they can assess the equity and inclusiveness of their hiring practices, rules, and procedures. To give further training and support, organisations can collaborate with external consultants or organisations that specialise in diversity and inclusion.

Finally, workplace stigma can have a substantial influence on both individuals and organisations. Discrimination and exclusion can impair productivity, lower morale, and increase turnover rates. Furthermore, people who are stigmatised are more likely to suffer from anxiety, sadness, and other mental health issues. Organisations, on the other hand, can try to alleviate the impact of stigma in the workplace and create a more inviting and diverse workplace by developing a culture of inclusivity and respect, addressing structural challenges, and providing resources and assistance.

Ways to tackle workplace stigma

This topic will go through several strategies for dealing with stigma in the workplace.

- **Educate yourself and others:**Educating yourself and others is the first step in overcoming stigma. This entails becoming acquainted with various cultures, beliefs, disabilities, and mental health concerns. It also entails educating yourself on the many types of workplace stigma. You can educate people and attempt to change attitudes and behaviours once you have a better grasp of the challenges.

- **Create an inclusive culture:**Creating an inclusive culture entails making sure that everyone feels welcome and respected in the workplace. This can be accomplished by promoting diversity and inclusion, giving cultural sensitivity training, and encouraging open communication. You may help to lessen the stigma in the workplace by fostering a safe and welcoming environment.

- **Implement rules and processes:**It is critical to have policies and procedures in place that address workplace discrimination and harassment. This includes anti-discrimination policies based on race, gender, handicap, and sexual orientation. All employees should be made aware of these regulations, and any infractions should be dealt with swiftly and fairly.

- **Provide support and resources:**Employees who are subjected to stigma or discrimination may require assistance and resources to cope with the situation. This can include access to counselling services, support groups, or disability accommodations. Making these materials available can help employees feel more supported and valued at work.

- **Lead by example:**Workplace leaders must set the tone for the workplace culture by setting a good example. This entails fostering diversity and treating everyone with dignity and respect. Leaders can also take action to address any incidents of stigma or discrimination that come to their attention.

To summarise, fighting stigma in the workplace necessitates a collaborative effort from everyone in the organisation. We can establish a welcoming and supportive workplace for all employees by educating ourselves and others, developing a culture of inclusivity, enacting rules and procedures, giving support and resources, and leading by example.

Workplace mental health promotion

Mental health is an important component of overall well-being because it influences all aspects of a person's life, including their job life. Unfortunately, mental health issues are frequently disregarded in the workplace, resulting in bad outcomes for both employees and employers. Employers can take numerous initiatives to help their employees' well-being in order to enhance mental health in the workplace.

The first step in boosting mental wellness in the workplace is to foster an open communication culture. Employees should feel free to discuss their mental health concerns with coworkers and managers without fear of discrimination or reprisal. Employers may help by providing mental health awareness training and resources, as well as promoting open discussions about mental health issues.

Access to mental health services is another strategy to boost mental health in the workplace. Employee assistance programmes (EAPs), counselling services, and other resources that employees can use to get help when they need it are examples of this. Employers can also collaborate with mental health professionals to offer educational seminars and workshops on stress management, mindfulness, and other approaches to assist employees in managing their mental health.

Employers can take action to reduce workplace stress in addition to offering access to mental health services. Creating a flexible work schedule, allowing employees to work from home, and providing adequate time off for relaxation and rehabilitation are all examples of this. Employers should also encourage healthy behaviours like exercise, good food, and adequate sleep to assist employees in managing their stress levels.

Addressing workplace bullying and harassment is another strategy to boost mental health in the workplace. These behaviours can have a negative impact on mental health and lead to anxiety, sadness, and other problems. Employers should have clear rules in place to manage workplace bullying and harassment, and any reported incidences should be addressed as soon as possible.

Finally, by creating a healthy work environment, businesses can enhance mental health in the workplace. This can involve recognising and rewarding employee accomplishments, offering opportunities for professional advancement, and instilling a sense of community and belonging in employees. Employers can also establish a positive workplace culture by encouraging social activities and team-building exercises.

Finally, fostering mental health in the workplace is critical for employee well-being and organisational success. Employers may help their employees' mental health by promoting an open communication culture, giving access to mental health resources, lowering workplace stress, addressing workplace bullying and harassment, and fostering a happy work environment. Employers may help their employees succeed both personally and professionally by prioritising mental health in the workplace.

Employees have access to assistance and services

There has been a growing awareness of the impact of stigma on individuals and communities in recent years. Stigma in the workplace can have a significant impact on employees, leading to discrimination, social exclusion, and a variety of mental health difficulties. Fortunately, Stigma employees have access to a variety of help and services focused on supporting mental health and well-being and establishing a more inclusive and caring workplace atmosphere.

Employee assistance programmes (EAPs) are one of the most effective options accessible to Stigma employees. Employee assistance programmes (EAPs) are intended to offer employees access to a variety of support services, such as counselling, psychotherapy, and other forms of mental health treatment. EAPs are often provided to all employees as a free, confidential service that can be accessed online, over the phone, or in person.

Peer support groups are another useful resource for employees in Stigma. These groups are often conducted by employees who have faced stigma themselves, and they provide a safe and supportive atmosphere for employees to discuss their experiences, seek advice, and connect with others who are facing similar issues. Employees who feel alone or alone in their experiences with stigma may benefit from peer support groups.

Aside from EAPs and peer support groups, many organisations provide training and education programmes to help employees understand the nature of stigma and how to establish a more inclusive and supportive workplace culture. These programmes may consist of workshops, seminars, or online courses covering themes such as unconscious bias, cultural competency, and mental health awareness.

Finally, it's worth noting that many Stigma employees may benefit from individualised support from their employers. Flexible work hours, job sharing, or remote work arrangements may be included, as well as access to medical leave or disability benefits.

Finally, Stigma workers have access to a wide range of services and support targeted at enhancing mental health and well-being and establishing a more inclusive and friendly workplace atmosphere. Employees who use these resources can better deal with the issues of stigma and achieve greater success and fulfilment in their personal and professional life.

Chapter 6 Getting Around Stigma in Healthcare

The impact of stigma on healthcare

Stigmatisation can lead to discrimination, exclusion, and marginalisation, all of which can have serious consequences for individuals and communities health and well-being.

Stigma in healthcare can create barriers to accessing services, delay diagnosis and treatment, and drive patients to avoid seeking care entirely. Stigmatised diseases including mental illness, substance misuse, and HIV/AIDS are frequently associated with shame, guilt, and fear, which can deter people from getting care.

Stigma can also have an impact on the quality of care provided to patients. Certain patient populations may be stigmatised by healthcare practitioners, which can lead to unfavourable attitudes and behaviours such as refusal to offer care, dismissiveness, or lack of empathy. As a result, stigmatised patients may receive inadequate or improper treatment, resulting in lower health outcomes.

Individuals and communities' mental health can also be impacted by stigma. Stigmatisation causes stress and isolation, which can lead to anxiety, sadness, and other mental health issues. Internalised shame and guilt associated with stigmatised disorders can further exacerbate mental health difficulties and make it more difficult for people to seek care.

Stigma can also lead to social and economic inequality, exacerbating health inequities. Stigmatised groups are frequently subjected to discrimination in school, work, and housing, limiting their access to services that promote health and well-being.

Education and awareness campaigns, cultural competence training for healthcare personnel, and advocacy for policies that promote equality and inclusion are all part of efforts to overcome stigma in healthcare. Encourage patients to share their experiences and seek aid from peers and support groups to alleviate the isolation and shame associated with stigmatised conditions.

Finally, stigma has a profound impact on healthcare, influencing access to care, care quality, mental health, and social and economic equality. Combating stigma is critical to enhancing health and well-being for all individuals and communities, as well as eliminating health disparities. Recognising the negative impacts of stigma and working to create a more inclusive and supportive environment for all is critical for healthcare practitioners, legislators, and society as a whole.

Recognising Stigma in Healthcare Settings

Stigma is a widespread issue in healthcare, and it can have serious effects on patients' physical and mental health results.

Here are some pointers on how to spot stigma in healthcare settings:

- **Take note of the terminology used by healthcare providers:**Healthcare practitioners' language can indicate a lot about their views towards patients. Providers who use stigmatising language may be unaware of the effect their words have on patients. Look for phrases that imply judgement, blaming, or stereotyping. A provider, for example, who refers to a patient with a substance use issue as a "drug addict" is employing stigmatising language.

- **Examine treatment disparities:**Stigma can lead to unequal treatment in healthcare settings. people with mental health problems, for example, may be given less time with their healthcare practitioner or prescribed different, less effective medications than people without mental health problems. Examine patterns of disparate care and speak with patients about their experiences.

- **Examine how healthcare providers treat patients:**Stigma can also be seen in how healthcare providers deal with their patients. Patients may be treated with less empathy and respect by providers who have stigmatising attitudes. A healthcare provider, for example, who rolls their eyes or sighs when a patient with a mental health illness recounts their symptoms is engaging in stigmatising behaviour.

- **Inquire about patients' experiences:**Patients are frequently the finest source of information on stigma in healthcare settings. Inquire about patients' experiences with healthcare providers, and take note of any comments that imply stigmatising attitudes or behaviour. Patients may be afraid to speak up about stigma, therefore it is critical to provide a secure and supportive atmosphere for them to do so.

- **Keep an eye out for nonverbal clues:**Nonverbal indicators can disclose stigmatising attitudes and behaviours. A healthcare provider, for example, who avoids eye contact with a patient who has a mental health illness or makes dismissive gestures may be engaging in stigmatising behaviour. Pay attention to nonverbal signs and patterns of behaviour that may indicate stigma.

Finally, recognising stigma in healthcare settings is critical for improving patient outcomes and establishing a more equal healthcare system. We can identify and remove stigma in healthcare settings by listening to healthcare providers' words, searching for inequalities in treatment, seeing how patients are treated, interviewing patients about their experiences, and watching for nonverbal clues. Because stigma can be subtle and unconscious, it is critical to be watchful and continue to educate healthcare providers about the impact of stigma on patients.

Techniques for advocating for yourself in medical contexts

Advocating for yourself in healthcare environments can be difficult, particularly when stigma is present. Stigma can create hurdles to healthcare access, making it harder to obtain the care you require. There are, however, measures you can employ to advocate for yourself in hospital environments where stigma exists.

- **Educate yourself:**Educating yourself on your disease is one of the most critical things you can do to advocate for yourself in healthcare settings. Learn everything you can about your diagnosis, treatment choices, and drugs. This knowledge will empower you to ask informed questions and make informed decisions regarding your health care.

- **Raise your voice:**Speaking up in hospital settings can be scary, especially if you feel judged or stigmatised. However, keep in mind that you have the right to ask questions and share your concerns. Be specific and forceful about what you require and expect from your healthcare providers.

- **Bring an advocate:**It can be beneficial to bring someone with you to medical appointments. This could be a family member, a friend, or a professional advocate. An advocate can offer emotional support, assist you in remembering questions you wish to ask, and provide an impartial viewpoint on your care.

- **Use non-stigmatizing language:**Stigmatising language is damaging and can obstruct good communication with healthcare practitioners. Use person-first language, which means you prioritise the person over their diagnosis or illness. Instead of stating "a diabetic," say "a person with diabetes." This contributes to the reduction of stigma and the promotion of more respectful and empathetic dialogue.

- **Locate supportive healthcare providers:**Not all healthcare professionals are created equal, and some may be more stigmatising than others. Look for providers that understand your situation and treat you with respect and sensitivity. If you are not happy with your current provider, consider switching to a more supportive physician.

Finally, advocating for yourself in healthcare environments can be difficult when stigma is present. You may improve your chances of receiving the care you need and deserve by educating yourself, speaking up, bringing an advocate, using non-stigmatizing language, and finding supportive healthcare practitioners. Remember that regardless of your diagnosis or condition, you have the right to be treated with dignity and respect.

There are resources and help available for persons who are experiencing stigma in healthcare:

Individuals seeking healthcare treatments may face substantial stigma. Stigma is defined as a negative attitude or belief about a specific group of people, such as those suffering from a specific condition, substance use problem, or mental illness. This stigma can result in discrimination, decreased access to care, and poorer health outcomes for people who are afflicted. However, services and help are available for anyone who is experiencing stigma in healthcare.

To begin, one can seek assistance from patient advocacy organisations. These organisations are committed to assisting those living with certain conditions with information and support. They can also assist people in navigating the healthcare system, connecting them with healthcare professionals, and providing emotional support. The National Alliance on Mental Illness (NAMI), the American Diabetes Association, and the National Organisation for Rare Disorders are a few examples of such organisations.

Second, healthcare providers can give those experiencing stigma support and information. Many healthcare personnel have received training in dealing with stigma and can work with patients to identify any barriers to care. To combat the emotional burden of stigma, providers might also refer clients to support groups or counselling programmes. Furthermore, healthcare providers can educate themselves on the various problems that diverse communities may experience when it comes to receiving healthcare services.

Third, community-based organisations can provide those confronting stigma with assistance and services. These organisations may give healthcare information, assist with transportation to medical visits, and provide social support. Community health centres, faith-based organisations, and LGBTQ+ advocacy groups are examples of such organisations.

Finally, government institutions can provide assistance to persons who face stigma in the healthcare system. The Substance Abuse and Mental Health Services Administration (SAMHSA), for example, offers information on mental health and substance use disorder treatment services, as well as resources for locating healthcare professionals. Health disparities and how to overcome them are addressed by the Centres for Disease Control and Prevention (CDC).

To summarise, stigma can be a substantial obstacle for people seeking healthcare. There are, however, resources and support available to assist individuals in overcoming these challenges. Patient advocacy organisations, healthcare professionals, community-based organisations, and government agencies can all help persons experiencing stigma in healthcare by giving support and services. We can assist ensure that everyone gets access to the care they require and deserve by working together.

Chapter 7 Stigma and Personal Relationships

Stigma's Influence on Relationships

Stigma is a powerful force that can influence how we perceive and treat people. It is described as people's negative attitudes and opinions against a specific group or individual based on perceived distinctions or features. Stigma can have far-reaching consequences, affecting everything from mental health to social connections. In this topic, we will look at how stigma affects relationships and how to overcome it.

Stigma can take various forms, ranging from racial prejudice to gender-based prejudice, and it can have a significant impact on the quality of relationships. Individuals who are stigmatised, for example, may struggle to form and maintain good relationships as a result of unfavourable preconceptions and prejudice. They may feel rejected, alone, and unsupported by their peers, which can contribute to feelings of loneliness and low self-esteem.

In partnerships, stigma can also create hurdles to communication and understanding. People who have negative sentiments towards a specific group or individual may be less likely to engage in open and honest discourse.

Misunderstandings, miscommunications, and a breakdown in trust can result, in exacerbating the harmful impacts of stigma on relationships.

Furthermore, stigma can be particularly damaging in intimate relationships. Individuals who are stigmatised may find it difficult to find partners who accept them for who they are, leading to feelings of rejection and shame. They may also feel more anxious and stressed as they worry about being judged or discriminated against by their relationships.

Even while stigma has a negative impact on relationships, there are strategies to overcome it. Education on the detrimental impacts of stigma is one of the most essential things we can do for ourselves and others. We may begin to confront and break down preconceptions and prejudices by raising knowledge and understanding of the challenges, promoting a more inclusive and accepting society.

Another critical stage is to develop empathy and compassion for persons who are stigmatised. This includes listening to their stories, offering support and understanding, and treating them with dignity and respect. We can achieve this by creating a secure and welcoming environment in which everyone may thrive and form meaningful relationships.

Finally, stigma is a powerful force that can have a significant impact on relationships. It can stifle dialogue and understanding, foster emotions of rejection and isolation, and erode the trust and intimacy required for good partnerships. We can, however, overcome the negative impacts of stigma and develop healthier, more inclusive relationships by raising awareness, fostering empathy and compassion, and confronting stereotypes and prejudices.

Relationship Stigma Reduction Techniques

Stigma is a social construct defined as a negative attribute or stereotype attached to a group of individuals or specific behaviour. It can take many forms, including discrimination, prejudice, and social isolation. Stigma can be especially difficult in partnerships since it can obstruct communication, trust, and intimacy.

There are, however, measures that can be used to overcome stigma in relationships and develop healthy, productive partnerships.

- **Educate Both You and Your Partner:**Education is one of the most successful techniques for reducing stigma in partnerships. Take the time to educate yourself on the stigma that your spouse is subjected to, including its causes, effects, and prevalence. Learn about how stigma can affect a person's mental and emotional health, as well as how it can create hurdles to communication, trust, and intimacy. Share your understanding with your partner and encourage them to do the same.

- **Dispel Stigma and Discrimination:**Fighting stigma and discrimination is a vital step towards overcoming its negative consequences. Speak out against unfavourable attitudes and prejudices in your personal and professional life, as well as in your community. Confront those who make harsh or insulting remarks and educate them on the consequences of their words. Encourage your partner to do the same, and lend your support to their efforts to combat stigma.

- **Create a Support System:**Creating a support network is critical for overcoming stigma in partnerships. Friends, family members, and professionals who understand and support your relationship can all be included. Surrounding yourself with positive and accepting people can assist to mitigate the harmful impacts of stigma and prejudice. Seeking help from mental health specialists can also help you cope with the emotional burden of stigma.

- **Communicate honestly and openly:**Communication that is open and honest is essential for overcoming stigma in partnerships. Discuss the difficulties that stigma brings with your partner, and work together to find solutions. Encourage your partner to share their emotions and sentiments, and validate their feelings. When communication is open and honest, it can aid in the development of trust and intimacy, both of which are necessary for good partnerships.

- **Concentrate on the Positive:**Keeping the positive features of your relationship in mind can assist to mitigate the negative consequences of stigma. Celebrate your love and commitment to each other, and concentrate on the aspects of your relationship that make it unique. Put an emphasis on your shared beliefs, interests, and goals, and collaborate to achieve them. By concentrating on the positive qualities of your relationship, you can lay a solid basis for overcoming stigma and establishing a healthy, positive connection.

Finally, stigma can cause substantial difficulties in partnerships. There are, however, measures that can be used to combat stigma and create healthy, beneficial connections. You can overcome stigma and develop a healthy, resilient relationship by educating yourself and your partner, addressing stigma and prejudice, creating a support system, speaking openly and honestly, and concentrating on the good.

Communicating about mental health with family and friends

Mental health is an important element of general well-being, and it's necessary to talk about it openly and honestly, especially with loved ones. However, discussing mental health with those closest to us may be difficult and frequently uncomfortable. Regardless, it is critical to have these dialogues in order to receive the required support and treatment.

Here are some suggestions for talking about mental health with loved ones:

- **Choose a safe and comfortable space:**Make sure you choose a location where you and your loved one feel at ease and safe. It may be a peaceful room or a park where you can both go for a walk. Making the surroundings comfortable can help to alleviate tension and stress during the conversation.

- **Be truthful and direct:**When discussing mental health difficulties, it is critical to be truthful and direct. Don't try to sugarcoat the situation or minimise your emotions. Speak frankly and honestly about your difficulties and emotions. Remember that your loved one may be unaware of the magnitude of your mental health challenges, so be honest about your feelings.

- **Listen to what they have to say:**communication is a two-way street. Listen to your loved one's point of view, especially if they have worries or questions regarding your mental health. Try to be receptive to their feedback and point of view, and keep in mind that they may not fully get your experiences.

- **Educate them:**It is critical to educate your loved ones on mental illness and mental health. Give them resources and information on your illness so they can better comprehend what you're going through. This can help to reduce some of their anxiety and confusion about mental health.

- **Request assistance:**Inform your loved one that you require their assistance and attention. Don't be afraid to ask for assistance, whether it's emotional support, practical assistance, or assistance in obtaining professional therapy. It's normal to ask for help, and having a solid support system may make or break your mental health journey.

- **Please be patient:**Remember that discussing mental health can be difficult for both you and your loved one. It is critical to be patient and empathetic, as well as to allow your loved one to process their thoughts and emotions. Be prepared for the talk to last and for both of you to feel comfortable discussing your mental health honestly.

To summarise, communicating with loved ones about mental health can be difficult, but it is critical to have these talks. Remember to choose a safe and comfortable environment, to be honest, and straightforward, to listen to their point of view, to educate them, to ask for help, and to be patient. You can create a solid support system and get the care and assistance you need to manage your mental health if you take the correct approach.

Developing positive and helpful connections

One of the most essential things we can do for our mental and emotional well-being is to cultivate good and supportive connections. Relationships are an important element of our life since they may provide us with so much joy and fulfilment. Building robust, supportive, and healthy connections, on the other hand, can be difficult, especially in today's fast-paced and frequently isolated society.

We will look at some advice and tactics for developing healthy and supportive relationships on this topic.

- **Communicate Effectively:**The foundation of any healthy relationship is effective communication. Misunderstandings and confrontations can arise in the absence of effective communication. As a result, it is critical to engage in open, honest, and respectful conversations with the individuals in our lives. This includes actively listening to others, clearly expressing oneself, and refraining from passive-aggressive behaviour.

- **Be Empathetic:**Empathy is the ability to comprehend and share the emotions of others. Being empathic allows us to connect with people on a deeper level and demonstrate our concern for their well-being. It also makes us more understanding and patient when disagreements emerge. To be more sympathetic, consider seeing yourself in the shoes of the other person and imagining how they could be experiencing. Then, with kindness and compassion, answer.

- **Respect Boundaries:**Boundaries are the restrictions we set for ourselves and others in order to protect our mental and physical well-being. It is critical to respect the boundaries of others while also clearly communicating our own. This contributes to the development of a sense of safety and trust in our relationships, as well as the avoidance of misunderstandings and conflicts.

- **Support Each Other:**Supporting one another is an important aspect of developing healthy and helpful relationships. Supporting one another improves our bonds and creates trust, whether it's providing emotional support during a tough time or assisting with practical duties like running errands. It is also critical to recognise and appreciate each other's victories and accomplishments, as this contributes to a healthy and supportive environment.

- **Resolve Conflicts Healthyly:**Conflicts are an inevitable element of any relationship. To avoid hurting the relationship, it is critical to settle arguments in a healthy manner. This entails avoiding blaming and criticism, actively listening to one another, and working together to find a solution that works for both sides. It is also critical to apologies when appropriate and to forgive one another when mistakes are made.

To summarise, developing healthy and supportive relationships takes time and effort, but it is well worth it. We may develop relationships that bring us joy and fulfilment by practising good communication, empathy, respecting boundaries, supporting one another, and resolving problems in a healthy manner. Remember that relationships are an important component of our lives and are worth investing in.

Chapter 8 Promoting Good Mental Health

The significance of good mental health

Mental health is an important aspect of overall well-being. It influences our thoughts, feelings, and behaviors, and it can have a considerable impact on our quality of life. Positive mental health is essential for coping with stress, making healthy decisions, and maintaining rewarding relationships. We shall address the significance of positive mental health and its advantages in this topic.

What exactly is Positive Mental Health?

Positive mental health is a condition of well-being that allows people to reach their full potential, manage life's regular pressures, work efficiently, and give back to their community. It entails being able to control emotions, form healthy relationships, and keep a happy attitude in life. Positive mental health is defined as the existence of positive feelings, attitudes, and behaviors that contribute to feelings of enjoyment, fulfillment, and contentment.

Advantages of Positive Mental Health

- **Improved Physical Health:**Individuals with good mental health have superior physical health results, according to research. They are less likely to develop chronic diseases such as heart disease, diabetes, and stroke. Positive mental health is also linked to greater immune system function, better sleep quality, and living a longer life.

- **Improved Relationships:**Good mental health is associated with good relationships. Individuals with good mental health can communicate more effectively, overcome issues, and build meaningful connections with others. They are also more likely to be in satisfying love relationships and have robust social support networks.

- **Increased Resilience:**Positive mental health aids in the development of resilience, or the ability to recover from adversity. Individuals with positive mental health are better able to cope, learn from their experiences, and adapt to new conditions when faced with obstacles or disappointments.

- **Improved Work Performance:**Positive mental health is associated with improved work performance. People who have good mental health are more productive, creative, and engaged at work. They are also more likely to enjoy job satisfaction and achieve career success.

- **Improved Overall Well-being:**Overall Improvement Positive mental health contributes to overall well-being, which includes the physical, emotional, social, and spiritual aspects of health. It fosters a sense of meaning, purpose, and fulfillment in life, which can lead to increased happiness and fulfillment.

How to Encourage Good Mental Health, Individuals can encourage positive mental health in a variety of ways:

- **Practice Self-care:**Self-care activities such as exercise, meditation, and relaxation techniques can help you manage stress and increase mental well-being.

- **Build Resilience:**Develop Coping Skills, Positive Self-Talk, and Problem-Solving Skills: Developing coping skills, positive self-talk, and problem-solving skills can help build resilience and enhance mental health.

- **Maintain Healthy Relationships:**Maintaining healthy relationships with friends, family, and romantic partners can improve mental health results.

- **Seek Professional Treatment When Needed:**Seeking professional treatment from a mental health expert when experiencing signs of mental illness helps prevent symptoms from worsening and improve mental health outcomes.

Finally, positive mental health is critical for general well-being. It gives people the tools they need to deal with stress, create healthy relationships, and achieve their goals. Individuals can improve their quality of life and enjoy greater pleasure and fulfillment by encouraging positive mental health through self-care, resilience-building, and getting help when needed.

Methods for Improving Mental Health

Mental health is an important component of overall well-being. It is defined as a state of well-being in which an individual recognizes his or her own abilities, can manage typical life challenges, works productively, and can contribute to his or her community. Unfortunately, mental health problems are becoming more prevalent in today's culture. In fact, it is projected that one in every four people will suffer from a mental health problem at some point in their lives.

There are, thankfully, measures that may be used to help enhance mental health. These tactics are applicable to anyone, regardless of whether they have a mental health diagnosis. **Here are some of the most effective mental health strategies:**

- **Exerciseregularly:**Regular exercise has been proven to be an excellent method of lowering stress, anxiety, and depression. Endorphins, which are natural mood boosters, are released during exercise. It also aids in the improvement of self-esteem, energy levels, and sleep quality.

- **Practice mindfulness:**Mindfulness is a strategy that requires paying attention to the current moment without judgment. It can assist to reduce stress and anxiety, as well as boost mood and resilience. Mindfulness can be practiced in a variety of methods, including meditation, yoga, and deep breathing techniques.

- **Get enough sleep:**Sleep is necessary for mental wellness. Sleep deprivation can cause irritation, mood fluctuations, and difficulties concentrating. To increase sleep quality, aim for at least 7-8 hours of sleep per night and maintain a consistent sleep regimen.

- **Eat a healthy diet:**A healthy, well-balanced diet can help to boost mood and overall well-being. A diet heavy in processed foods, sweets, and saturated fats can cause lethargy and irritability. Eat a diet high in fruits and vegetables, healthy grains, and lean protein sources.

- **Connect with others:**Social support is essential for mental wellness. Spending time with friends and family, joining a social group or club, and volunteering can all help to lift one's spirits and alleviate feelings of isolation.

- **Practice self-care:**Self-care entails making time for activities that are joyful and gratifying. Hobbies, reading, having a bath, or anything else that helps you rest and unwind can be included. Self-care can assist to alleviate stress and enhance overall health.

- **Seek professional help:**It is critical to get professional help if you are suffering chronic symptoms of melancholy, anxiety, or other mental health difficulties. A mental health expert can assist you in developing coping techniques, providing support, and, if necessary, prescribing medication.

Finally, there are numerous ways that can be used to help promote mental health. You may help to reduce stress, boost mood, and increase resilience by adopting these tactics into your everyday routine. Remember that excellent mental health is vital for total well-being, and improving your mental health is an investment in your future happiness and success.

Increasing resilience and coping abilities

We will all confront problems and barriers in our lives. Some may be little, while others may be major and life-changing. When faced with adversity, it is critical to developing resilience and coping abilities in order to sustain mental health and well-being.

Resilience is the ability to recover from misfortune and deal with life's difficulties. It is not a natural ability, but rather a skill that may be cultivated by deliberate practice. Coping skills, on the other hand, are the approaches and strategies we employ to deal with stress and preserve emotional equilibrium.

Here are some strategies for building resilience and coping skills:

- **Practice self-care:**It is vital to take care of yourself physically, emotionally, and psychologically in order to create resilience. This involves eating a nutritious diet, getting adequate sleep, and exercising regularly. Taking time for yourself, participating in hobbies or activities you enjoy, and getting help when required are all important.

- **Develop a growth mindset:**A growth mentality views setbacks and challenges as chances for growth and learning. Rather than being defeated by failure, folks with a growth mindset view it as an opportunity to learn and try again.

- **Learn relaxation techniques:**Deep breathing, meditation, and yoga are all relaxation strategies that can help reduce stress and enhance resilience. These practices can be used on a daily basis to assist establish a sense of serenity and balance.

- **Build a support system:**In stressful circumstances, having a supportive network of friends, family, or a therapist can bring a sense of stability and comfort. It is critical to seek assistance when necessary and to surround yourself with positive influences.

- **Set realistic goals:**Setting attainable goals can aid in the development of confidence and resilience. Failure can lead to emotions of inadequacy and defeat when goals are set too high. Setting realistic goals and appreciating minor victories along the road can aid in the development of resilience and motivation.

- **Practice gratitude:**Practising thankfulness and focusing on the positive things in life can help you build resilience and manage stress. Recognizing and appreciating the positive aspects of life can assist in shifting attention away from negative thoughts and feelings.

- **Embrace change:**Change is unavoidable, and learning to adjust to new circumstances is critical for developing resilience. Accepting change and seeing it as an opportunity for growth can aid in the development of resilience and coping abilities.

Finally, establishing resilience and coping skills is critical for sustaining mental health and well-being in the face of hardship. Anyone can build these talents and learn to cope with life's obstacles with deliberate practice. We may build resilience and thrive in the face of hardship by concentrating on self-care, developing a support system, setting realistic goals, and practicing thankfulness.

Finding life's meaning and purpose

Finding meaning and purpose in life has been a fundamental human search for generations. From ancient philosophers to contemporary thinkers, people have strived to comprehend the meaning of their lives and the purpose of their existence. While the answer is obviously subjective and personal, there are certain universal truths that can guide us in our pursuit of a full life.

Exploring our values and beliefs is one of the first steps toward finding meaning and purpose in life. Our values define what we value in life, whereas our beliefs form our perception of the world and our place in it. We can obtain a better knowledge of our inner selves and what motivates us to live a fulfilled life by evaluating our values and beliefs.

Setting meaningful goals is another crucial component in finding meaning and purpose in life. Goals provide us with a sense of direction and purpose, as well as a sense of achievement and satisfaction when we achieve them. However, it is critical that our goals are consistent with our values and beliefs, as pursuing goals that contradict our basic principles can lead to feelings of discontent and unhappiness.

In addition to creating meaningful goals, cultivating a sense of thankfulness and appreciation for the current moment is essential. We may find significance and purpose in even the most boring elements of life by focusing on the present moment and recognizing the beauty and worth in everyday occurrences.

Connecting with others and developing meaningful connections is another important part of finding meaning and purpose in life. Humans are social beings, and the quality of our connections has a significant impact on our sense of well-being. We can build a sense of belonging and connection by nurturing our relationships with family, friends, and other loved ones, which can provide us with a deep sense of meaning and purpose.

Finally, it is critical to participate in activities that bring us joy and fulfillment. Finding activities that connect with our values and beliefs, whether through a hobby or volunteer work, can help us find purpose and meaning in our lives.

In conclusion, discovering our life's meaning and purpose is a personal and continuing process that necessitates self-reflection, goal-setting, gratitude, meaningful relationships, and participation in things that offer us joy and fulfillment. We can find a feeling of purpose and fulfillment in our lives by adopting these values and living a life that is genuinely worth living.

Chapter 9 Creating Community Support

The Community's Role in Mental Health

Mental health is an important element of our well-being, and it must be maintained. The human mind is a complicated entity that can be influenced by a variety of elements such as heredity, environment, and lifestyle. However, one critical factor that is sometimes overlooked is the function of the community in mental health. A community can offer many sorts of support, ranging from emotional to practical assistance, to persons dealing with mental health issues.

The community's role in mental health is diverse. For starters, it can offer a sense of belonging and social support. Individuals who are solitary or lonely are more likely to suffer mental health problems such as depression and anxiety. A strong sense of community, on the other hand, can help overcome these sensations. Having a supportive network of people around you can help you feel appreciated, accepted, and understood, which can lead to better mental health outcomes.

Additionally, communities can provide practical assistance, such as access to resources and services. Mental health services, such as counselling and therapy, can be costly and out of reach for certain people. Communities, on the other hand, can give resources and information on low-cost or free mental health services, making them available to individuals in need.

Promoting healthy habits is another important responsibility of the community in mental health. A community can give opportunities for people to participate in physical activities, such as sports and fitness programmes, which can improve their mental health. Furthermore, communities can organise events and activities that promote healthy behaviours like eating healthily, getting enough sleep, and managing stress.

Communities can also help to reduce the stigma associated with mental health. Individuals seeking mental health services face substantial stigma. Communities, on the other hand, can educate folks about mental health issues and provide a secure, nonjudgmental atmosphere for those in need of assistance.

Furthermore, community involvement can give individuals an opportunity to engage in meaningful activities and acquire a sense of purpose. According to research, those who have a feeling of purpose are less likely to develop mental health problems. Volunteering or participating in meaningful activities in the community can help people discover a sense of purpose.

Finally, the importance of community in mental health cannot be emphasised. Communities can provide a sense of belonging, practical support, healthy lifestyle promotion, stigma reduction, and chances for individuals to participate in meaningful activities. As a result, it is critical to foster welcoming and inclusive communities that prioritise mental health and well-being. By doing so, we may create an environment in which people feel empowered and supported in dealing with mental health issues.

How to Build Compassionate Communities

Creating stigma-friendly communities is critical for encouraging social inclusion, eliminating discrimination, and increasing the quality of life for stigmatised people. In this topic, we will look at various techniques for developing stigma-friendly communities.

- **Education and Awareness:**Increased education and awareness are one of the most important tactics for developing stigma-friendly communities. Education promotes understanding and acceptance by debunking myths and assumptions about stigmatised groups. Workshops, seminars, and public events can educate people in the community. This can involve telling the tales of those who have been stigmatised or bringing specialists to speak on the effects of stigma on mental health and well-being. This can aid in the reduction of stigmatised persons' unfavourable attitudes and beliefs.

- **Empowerment and Support:**Another key strategy is to provide stigmatised persons with support and empowerment. This can involve forming support groups or peer networks to connect stigmatised persons with others who have gone through similar situations. These organisations can give a safe venue for people to share their tales, as well as emotional support and community building. Furthermore, community members can establish chances for stigmatised individuals to participate in communal decision-making and leadership roles. This can help to boost self-esteem and a sense of belonging.

- **Advocacy and Policy Change:**Advocacy and policy reform are critical strategies for achieving stigma-free communities. Members of the community can lobby for policy reforms that enhance social inclusion and decrease discrimination. This can involve advocating inclusive language and media representation, as well as supporting anti-discrimination laws and boosting access to mental health care. Members of the community can also collaborate with local governments and other organisations to develop awareness campaigns that encourage inclusion and minimise stigma.

- **Positive Language and Communication:**Positive language and communication are critical components in developing stigma-supportive cultures. Members of the community can choose to use language that is courteous, inclusive, and person-centred. This entails focusing on the individual rather than their stigmatised identity, as well as avoiding negative stereotypes or labels. Additionally, individuals in the community can promote constructive communication by emphasising active listening, empathy, and understanding.

- **Cultural Competence:**Finally, cultural competence is a key tool for developing stigma-supportive communities. This entails being aware of and respecting cultural variations and values that may influence how stigmatised people feel stigma. Members of the community can take measures to learn about various cultural perspectives and act to foster cultural sensitivity in the community. This can contribute to a more inviting and inclusive environment for all members of the community.

Finally, developing stigma-supportive communities is critical for encouraging social inclusion, eliminating discrimination, and improving the quality of life of stigmatised people. Community members can work to build a more inclusive and welcoming atmosphere for everybody through fostering education and awareness, empowerment and support, advocacy and policy reform, good language and communication, and cultural competence. It is critical that all members of the community collaborate to achieve this aim of creating a society that celebrates variety and respects the rights and dignity of all individuals.

Mental health services and support in the community

Mental health is a vital element of our general well-being, yet many people struggle to get the resources and help they require. For persons dealing with mental health concerns, there are a variety of community resources and support networks accessible. These services can provide individuals and their families with much-needed aid, guidance, and support.

Mental health clinics are one of the most essential community resources for mental health. Typically, these clinics are staffed by mental health specialists such as psychiatrists, psychologists, and therapists. They provide a variety of services, including mental health condition diagnosis and treatment, individual and group counselling, medication management, and crisis intervention. Many mental health clinics also offer information and support to relatives and loved ones of persons suffering from mental illnesses.

Another valuable resource for mental health support is support groups. These groups are typically made up of individuals who are going through similar experiences, and they offer a safe and supportive space for individuals to share their thoughts and feelings. Support groups can be particularly helpful for those who are coping with mental health issues such as depression, anxiety, or addiction.

Aside from mental health clinics and support groups, there are a variety of different community resources and support networks accessible to persons suffering from mental illnesses. Hotlines and crisis centres, for example, provide instant assistance and support to people in trouble. There are also community centres, churches, and other organisations in many communities that provide mental health support services such as counselling or treatment.

It is critical to remember that community resources and support systems are not one-size-fits-all. What works for one person might not work for another. It is critical to spend time investigating various resources and determining which ones work best for you. This may entail experimenting with various therapists, joining various support groups, or utilising various community services.

In addition to utilising community resources and support networks, individuals can take on a number of activities to improve their own mental health. These may include regular exercise, a balanced diet, adequate sleep, stress-reduction strategies such as meditation or yoga, and participation in activities that offer joy and fulfilment.

To summarise, mental health is an important component of total well-being, and there are several community services and support systems available to assist individuals and families dealing with mental health challenges. These tools can aid persons on the road to recovery and improve mental health by providing much-needed assistance, guidance, and support.

Overcoming social isolation and connecting with others

Humans are social creatures, and social interaction is a fundamental human need. In today's fast-paced society, however, social isolation is becoming more widespread. People frequently live in a state of loneliness, estranged from their friends, family, and community. Social isolation can have a negative impact on both mental and physical health, resulting in sadness, anxiety, and other health issues. As a result, it is critical to overcome social isolation and establish connections in order to live a full life.

Understanding the variables that contribute to social isolation is the first step towards resolving it. Living alone, working remotely, or relocating to a new place can all contribute to social isolation. Social isolation can also be caused by mental health issues such as anxiety or depression, which make it difficult to interact with others. The following stage is to take action in order to overcome social isolation.

Some tactics that may be useful are as follows:

- **Join groups and clubs:**Joining groups or clubs with similar interests can be a terrific way to meet new people and form new relationships. It might be a sports team, a reading club, or any other recreational organisation that you are interested in. This way, you can meet others who share your interests and establish new acquaintances more easily.

- **Volunteer:**Volunteering is a fantastic opportunity to meet new people and make a difference in your community. It can also provide people with a feeling of purpose and meaning in their lives. Volunteering at a local charity, hospital, or community centre is an option.

- **Attend social events:**Attending social gatherings might help you meet new people and form new friendships. You can go to events such as parties, concerts, and community gatherings. You might also try organising events with your friends or in your neighbourhood.

- **Join online communities:**Social media can be an excellent tool for connecting with people online. You can join online communities depending on your hobbies or interests. A Facebook group, an online forum, or any other social media platform can be used.

- **Reach out to people:**Reaching out to individuals can often be all that is required to make connections. You can contact old friends and family members by phone, text, or email. You can also try to connect with new people in your everyday life, such as coworkers or neighbours.

- **Seek professional help:**If you are experiencing social isolation as a result of a mental health problem such as anxiety or depression, it is critical that you get professional assistance. A therapist or counsellor can assist you in overcoming your mental health difficulties and provide you with coping methods to help you connect with others.

Finally, social isolation can have a significant influence on both mental and physical health. As a result, it is critical to overcome social isolation and establish contacts. You can develop meaningful relationships and live a fulfilling life by joining groups and clubs, volunteering, attending social events, joining online communities, reaching out to people, and seeking professional help. Remember that making connections takes time and effort, but the benefits are well worth it.

Chapter 10 Change Advocating

The effectiveness of Advocacy in eliminating the stigma

Stigma can also keep people from seeking care, whether it's for a mental health problem, a medical condition, or a social problem. Advocacy, on the other hand, is a powerful instrument that can help to combat stigma and encourage acceptance and understanding.

Advocacy is the use of one's voice to advocate a cause, generate awareness, and sway public opinion. Advocacy can take numerous forms, including public speaking, lobbying lawmakers, and submitting letters to the editor. Advocacy may be a powerful force for change when it comes to stigma.

Giving individuals a voice is one of the most essential ways that advocacy may help them overcome stigma. People who have faced stigma can assist to break down stereotypes and fight misconceptions by speaking out about their experiences. This can serve to foster empathy and understanding, as well as create a more supportive environment for persons who are stigmatized.

Advocacy can also assist in educating the public about the causes that contribute to stigma. For example, mental health stigma is frequently caused by a lack of knowledge about mental illness and how it affects people. Advocates can assist to minimise the fear and misunderstanding that can fuel stigma by educating others about mental health.

Advocacy can also help to bring about systemic change. Advocates can seek to create a more supportive atmosphere for persons impacted by stigma by pushing for policy changes or advocating for new legislation. Advocates may, for example, lobby for improved access to mental health services or for stricter safeguards against discrimination based on disability or sexual orientation.

Finally, advocating can enable persons who are stigmatized to have a feeling of community and belonging. Advocators can help to establish a sense of solidarity and support by bringing people together, which can be quite empowering. This can assist to alleviate the loneliness and humiliation that frequently accompany stigma, as well as creating a more positive and supportive environment for everyone.

Finally, advocacy is an effective method for combating stigma. Advocates can seek to break down stereotypes, challenge misconceptions, and promote acceptance and understanding by providing people a voice, educating the public, enacting systemic change, and cultivating a feeling of community. Advocacy may be a strong force for change, whether you are personally affected by stigma or simply wish to make a difference.

Ways to Participate in Mental Health Advocacy

Mental health has grown in relevance in today's culture, with more and more people recognizing the need of addressing mental health issues. Mental health advocacy is crucial in increasing awareness about mental health concerns as well as campaigning for greater care and resources for people in need.

Here are some ways to get involved in mental health advocacy if you are passionate about mental health and want to make a difference in your community:

- **Donate your time to mental health organizations:**Many mental health organizations rely on volunteers to assist with a variety of duties, including event planning, fundraising, and advocacy campaigns. Look for local mental health organizations in your region and inquire about volunteer possibilities.

- **Participate in mental health events:**Attending mental health events is an excellent way to learn more about mental health and meet others who share your commitment to mental health advocacy. Look for activities in your town such as mental health conferences, seminars, and workshops.

- **Share your story:**Sharing your personal mental health experiences can be a great approach to promoting awareness and combating stigma. You can tell your story on social media, at events, or even create a blog post or an article about it.

- **Propose policy modifications:**Changes in mental health policy can have a profound impact on the lives of those suffering from mental illnesses. Contacting your local lawmakers, signing petitions, and joining advocacy campaigns are all ways to push for legislative changes.

- **Support mental health initiatives:**Many businesses and organizations have implemented mental health initiatives to help their employees or society at large. You may help these programs by volunteering or giving to mental health organizations.

- **Educate yourself:**Understanding mental health is essential for effective advocacy. Read books, attend seminars, and take online courses to learn more about mental health and the challenges that people with mental illnesses face.

- **Participate in a mental health advocacy group:**There are numerous mental health advocacy groups you can join to network with like-minded people and push for better mental health assistance and resources.

Finally, mental health advocacy is a vital approach to supporting those who are suffering from mental illnesses and increasing awareness about mental health concerns in our community. You may make a meaningful impact in the lives of those suffering from mental illnesses by volunteering, attending events, sharing your story, pushing for legislative changes, supporting mental health programs, educating yourself, and joining advocacy groups.

Promoting policy change

To achieve social justice, equality, and human rights, it is critical to push for policy change in stigma. Advocating for policy change in stigma entails various processes, including raising awareness, doing research, forming coalitions, and developing policies. The first stage is to create public knowledge of stigma and its implications in order to mobilize public support and political will. This can be accomplished through media campaigns, public events, educational and training programs, and the participation of important stakeholders such as affected communities, activists, legislators, and opinion leaders.

The second phase is to do research to better understand the nature, origins, and effects of stigma, as well as to identify evidence-based remedies that may be used to drive policy development. This can include qualitative and quantitative research, surveys, focus groups, and literature reviews, as well as the participation of researchers, practitioners, and community people.

The third phase is to form coalitions and partnerships with stakeholders who share the goal of stigma reduction and social inclusion. Forming partnerships with advocacy groups, civil society organizations, healthcare providers, and other stakeholders, as well as engaging policymakers and politicians at all levels of government, can be part of this.

The third phase is to create and implement policies to combat stigma and prejudice that are based on evidence-based solutions and best practices. Legislation, rules, guidelines, and programs that promote social inclusion, diversity, and equity, as well as support and protection for individuals who are stigmatized and marginalized, can be included in these policies.

Advocating for policy change in stigma can be a difficult and complex process, requiring the removal of political, social, and cultural barriers. However, it is also a critical and rewarding endeavor, as it has the potential to enhance the lives of millions of individuals who face stigma and discrimination. We can create a more inclusive and compassionate society that values diversity and celebrates the complexity of human experience by advancing social justice, equality, and human rights.

Making society more inclusive and supportive

This can express as racism, sexism, homophobia, and ableism, among other things. Stigma creates barriers to social inclusion and has a negative influence on people's mental and physical health. To develop a more inclusive and supportive society, we must confront stigma at its source and endeavor to create a more welcoming and tolerant community.

To begin, raising awareness and educating people about the impact of stigma on individuals and society is critical. We may lessen fear, ignorance, and misconceptions by sharing factual information and refuting falsehoods. Education should be thorough and ongoing and should include activities aimed at schools, workplaces, and other community settings.

Second, we must actively encourage diversity and inclusion. Embracing diversity entails recognizing and appreciating the differences that make us distinct. This encompasses disparities in sexual orientation, gender identity, and ability, as well as cultural, linguistic, and religious distinctions. To promote diversity, equal opportunities must be provided, barriers to participation must be removed, and everyone must feel appreciated and respected.

Third, we must promote safe and supportive environments in which people can freely express themselves without fear of judgment or discrimination. This can be accomplished by establishing community groups, support networks, and online forums where people can share their stories and find comfort in knowing they are not alone. Individuals can benefit from emotional support, affirmation, and encouragement from these organizations, and they can also help to promote good change.

Fourth, we must fight to abolish discrimination in all aspects of society. Discrimination can manifest itself in a variety of ways, including employment, healthcare, education, housing, and criminal justice. To fight this, we must enact laws and regulations that encourage equitable access and opportunity for all people, regardless of background. It is also critical to hold individuals who discriminate accountable for their acts and to give victims reparation.

Finally, we must try to improve society's attitudes toward people who are stigmatized. This includes confronting negative preconceptions and prejudices, supporting positive role models, and recognizing and appreciating diversity. We must also ensure that those who are stigmatized have a say in the policies and practices that affect their life.

To summarise, developing a more inclusive and supportive society necessitates collective action on the part of individuals, groups, and institutions. We can establish a more tolerant and welcoming society where everyone can prosper by tackling stigma at its base, fostering diversity, creating safe places, eradicating discrimination, and altering cultural attitudes.

Conclusion

To summarise, overcoming the stigma associated with mental health and living a happy life is a difficult but attainable objective. Individual work, social support, and systemic change are all required. Individuals must prioritize their mental health by getting help when necessary, implementing good coping techniques, and engaging in self-care. Social support from family, friends, and mental health experts can also help someone overcome stigma and live a full life.

Furthermore, structural change is required to eliminate the stigma associated with mental health. Initiatives such as education and awareness campaigns to encourage understanding and acceptance of mental health concerns fall under this category. Employers, schools, and healthcare providers can all help to create safe and welcoming settings that prioritize mental health.

In conclusion, overcoming stigma and living a happy life is not a one-size-fits-all solution. Each person's path is unique and necessitates a customized strategy. However, by working together and establishing a caring and accepting community, we can all help to ensure that everyone has the opportunity to live a happy life free of the limits of mental health stigma.

www.ingramcontent.com/pod-product-compliance
Lightning Source LLC
LaVergne TN
LVHW091614170726
843492LV00007B/2398